# MARGRET & H.A.REY'S
# Curious George
## and the Firefighters

Illustrated in the style of H. A. Rey by Anna Grossnickle Hines

Houghton Mifflin Company  Boston

This is George.

He was a good little monkey and always very curious.

Today George and his friend the man with the yellow hat
joined Mrs. Gray and her class on their field trip to the fire station.

The Fire Chief was waiting for them right next to a big red fire truck.
"Welcome!" he said, and he led everyone upstairs to begin their tour.

There was a kitchen with a big table, and there were snacks for everyone. The Fire Chief told them all about being a firefighter. George tried hard to pay attention, but there were so many things for a little monkey to explore. Like that shiny silver pole in the corner. . . .

Where did that pole go? George was curious.

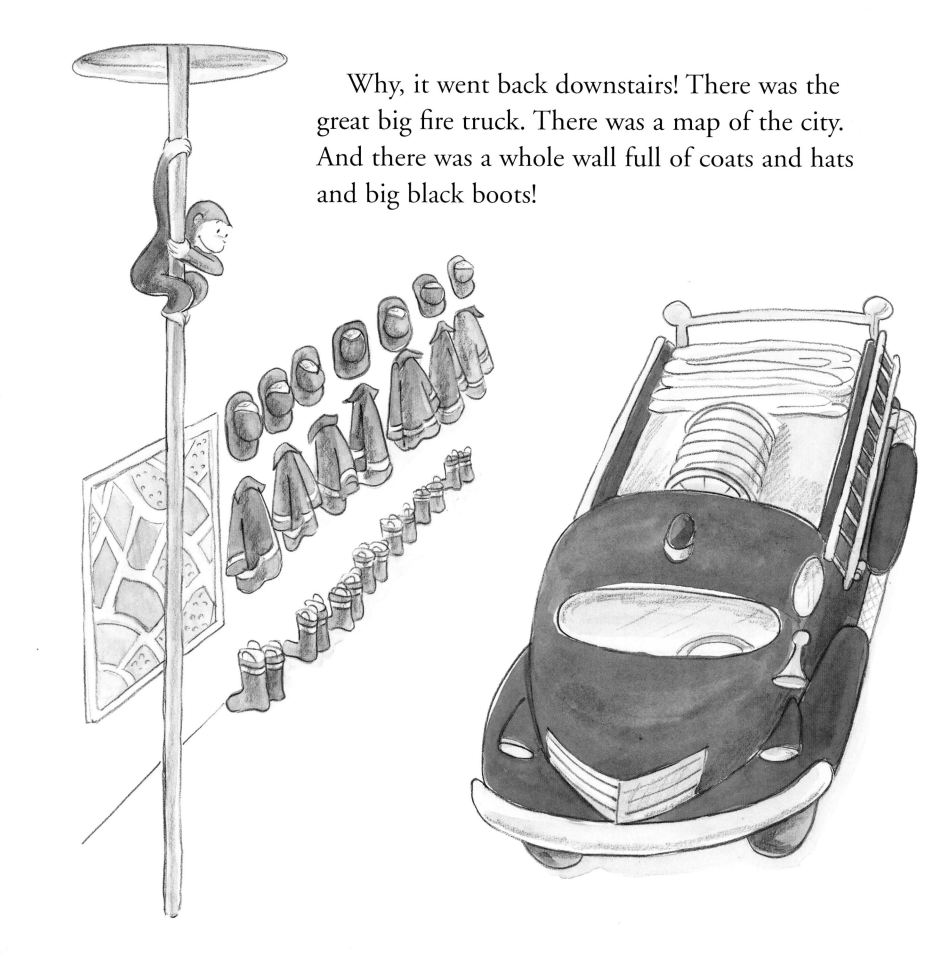

Why, it went back downstairs! There was the great big fire truck. There was a map of the city. And there was a whole wall full of coats and hats and big black boots!

George had an idea.
First he stepped into a
pair of boots.

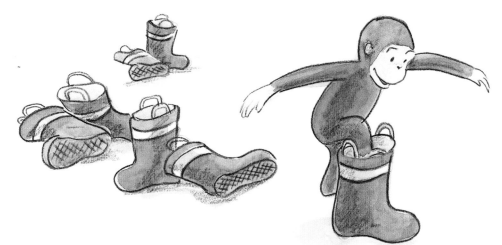

Next, he picked out a helmet.

And, finally, George put on a jacket.
He was a firefighter!

Suddenly . . . BRRRIINNGG!

The firefighters all rushed in.

"This is not my helmet!" said one.

"My boots are too big!" said another.

"Hurry! Hurry!" called the Fire Chief. A bright red light on the map of the city told him just where the fire was. There was no time to waste!

One by one, the firefighters jumped into the fire truck.

And so did George.

The fire truck with
all the firefighters sped
out of the firehouse.
And so did George!
The siren screamed and the lights flashed.

The truck turned right. Then it turned left.
"WHOO WHOO WHOO," went the whistle
and George held on tight.

And just like that the fire truck and all the firefighters pulled up to a pizza parlor on Main Street. Smoke was coming out of a window in the back and a crowd was gathering in the street.

"Thank goodness you're here!" cried the cook.

The firefighters rushed off the truck and started
unwinding their hoses. They knew just what to do.
And George was ready to help.
He climbed up on the hose reel. . . .

One of the firefighters saw George trying to help, and he
took George by the arm and led him out of the way.

"A fire is no place for a monkey!" he said to George. "You stay here
where it's safe."

George felt terrible.

George sat on the bench and looked around. Next to him on the ground was a bucket full of balls. George reached in and took one out. It fit in his hand just right, like the apple he'd had for a snack.

A little girl was watching
George. He tried to give her the
ball, but she was too frightened.

George took
another ball.

And another.
"Look," a boy said.
"That monkey is juggling!"

The boy took a ball from the cage and tossed it to George, but it went too high.

George climbed up onto the fire truck to get it.

Now George had four balls to juggle. He threw the balls higher and higher. He juggled with his hands. He juggled with his feet. He could do all kinds of tricks!

The boy threw another ball to George. George threw a ball back to the boy. The little girl reached down and picked up a ball, too. Soon all the children were throwing and catching, back and forth.

The Fire Chief came to tell everyone that the fire was out. Just then, the little girl laughed and said, "Look, Mommy—a fire monkey!"

"Hey!" called the Fire Chief. "What are you doing up there?"

"What a wonderful idea," the little girl's mother said to the Fire Chief. "Bringing this brave little monkey to help children when they're frightened."

"Oh," the Fire Chief said. "Well, er, thank you."

Before long the fire truck was back at the fire house, where a familiar voice called, "George!" It was the man with the yellow hat.

"This little monkey had quite an adventure," said one of the firefighters.

"Is everyone all right?" asked Mrs. Gray.

"Yes, it was just a small fire," said the Fire Chief.
"And George was a big help."
Now the field trip was coming to an end.
But there was one more treat in store. . . .

All the children got to take a ride around the neighborhood on the shiny red fire truck, and they each got their very own fire helmet. Even George! And it was just the right size for a brave little monkey.